THE ENCHANTED CARIBOU

"Magic Words", and the "Magic Words for Hunting Caribou" on page 10, were adapted and translated by Jerome Rothenberg. From *Shaking the Pumpkin: Traditional Poetry of the Indian North Americas*, edited with commentaries by Jerome Rothenberg (New York, Doubleday & Company, Inc., 1972).

LIBRARY OF CONGRESS CATALOGING IN PUBLICATION DATA

Cleaver, Elizabeth
  The enchanted caribou.

  Summary: A brave young hunter rescues a
maiden who has been changed into a white caribou.

  1. Indians of North America — Canada — Legends.
[1. Indians of North America — Canada — Legends]
I. Title.
E78.C2C59 1985   398.2'08997071   85-7465
ISBN 0-689-31170-2

Text and pictures copyright © 1985 by Elizabeth Cleaver
All rights reserved
Published in Canada by Oxford University Press, 1985
Printed and bound in Hong Kong by Scanner Art Services Inc., Toronto
First American Edition

MAGIC WORDS

In the very earliest time,
when both people and animals lived on earth,
a person could become an animal if he wanted to
and an animal could become a human being.
Sometimes they were people
and sometimes animals
and there was no difference.
All spoke the same language.
That was the time when words were like magic.
The human mind had mysterious powers.
A word spoken by chance
might have strange consequences.
It would suddenly come alive
and what people wanted to happen could happen—
all you had to do was say it.
Nobody could explain this:
That's the way it was.

THE ENCHANTED CARIBOU

ATHENEUM, NEW YORK, 1985

ELIZABETH CLEAVER

In the very earliest time, far away in a settlement by a northern lake, there lived a young woman called Tyya. She loved to wander alone collecting pieces of driftwood and caribou antlers to make dolls for children. As she walked she sang to herself and watched the gulls flap their wings in the clear air.

One day Tyya had wandered a long way from home when a heavy fog descended and she could see nothing in front of her.

Feeling lost and helpless, she sat down and wept.

After a few minutes something moved in the fog. Tyya was so frightened she stopped crying.

The figure came closer and closer.

Finally she could see what it was.

A young man!

When he spoke in a kindly voice, Tyya was no longer frightened.

"What are you doing here?" he asked.

"I was collecting driftwood when the fog descended," Tyya replied, "and I could see nothing in front of me. I am lost."

"Don't worry," he said. "I live close by with my two brothers. My name is Etosack. Come with me."

Tyya followed Etosack to his house, a summer tent made of caribou hides. She sat in front of a fire while Etosack served her caribou meat and broth and fresh berries. After her meal she felt warm and contented. With Etosack beside her, she gazed happily into the fire and watched the shadows it cast on the wall of the tent.

When the two brothers returned, they were surprised to find a beautiful woman sitting with Etosack.

"Who is she?" asked the first brother.

"How did she get here?" asked the second.

"She was lost in the fog," Etosack replied, "and I asked her to stay with us until tomorrow. Her name is Tyya."

The three brothers were hunters of caribou that roamed the tundra beyond the lake. Before lying down to sleep they performed a ceremonial dance to bring them success in the morning's hunt. First they put on caribou masks, and coats and boots of caribou skin. Then, to make music for their dance, one of them got out his caribou-skin drum and started beating on it. While the brothers danced around the fire, their shadows flickering against the wall of their tent, they chanted a magic hunting song:

> ". . . caribou-bou-bou.
> Put your footprints on this land —
> this land I'm standing on
> is rich with the plant food you love.
> See, I'm holding in my hand
> the reindeer moss you're dreaming of —
> so delicious, yum, yum, yum —
> Come, caribou, come."

Unable to resist the rhythmic drum beats, Tyya joined the brothers in their dance.

The drumming quickened, and the dancing quickened with it. Tossing their arms in the air as they leapt around the fire, the four dancers whirled faster and faster until they fell to the ground exhausted.

In the morning, before they set out for the hunt, the three brothers warned Tyya not to let anyone into their tent while they were away.

Left alone, Tyya took up a sharp knife and carved a piece of driftwood until a beautiful doll emerged. Then she made it a caribou-skin dress. While she sat working, someone came to the flap of the tent.

"Let me in," said an old woman's voice, "and give me a drink of water."

"I can't let you in," Tyya called. "This tent belongs to Etosack and his brothers. They have told me not to let anyone in while they are away."

The old woman replied crossly: "If you refuse to let me in, bad things will happen to you. I am a shaman."

A shaman! Tyya knew that a shaman had supernatural powers and could do terrible things. She let the woman in, forgetting what the brothers had told her.

After Tyya gave her a drink of water, the old woman said; "Now I will comb your hair," and she took out her magic ivory comb. As she drew it through the tangles in Tyya's hair, she started to sing:

"Ajaja, aja, aja, jaja . . ."

Tyya had never heard the melody before. It was so tender, so beautiful . . . She fell into a deep sleep, and the old woman crept away.

Tyya slept for many hours. When she woke and stretched her arms she felt herself being transformed.
Antlers slowly sprouted on her head, and her arms lengthened to legs. Her hands and feet became hooves.
She was no longer human.

Tyya had become a white caribou.
It trotted out of the tent and bounded across the tundra to join the herd.

That evening, when the brothers returned, they found that Tyya had gone. "Why would she leave without telling us?" asked Etosack unhappily, for he had fallen in love with Tyya.

That night Etosack had a dream about his dead grandmother, who had been a powerful shaman in her lifetime. She told him that Tyya had been changed into a white caribou by an evil shaman.

"Do what I tell you and you will have her back. In the morning take a feather, the bone and sinew of a caribou, a stone, and the doll that Tyya made. Then go out and look for the white caribou. When you find it, throw these things on its back and you will see what happens."

The next morning Etosack set out to find Tyya.

He walked for many hours until he spotted a caribou herd in the distance. Coming closer to it, he saw what he was looking for: the white caribou. He ran towards the herd shouting joyfully: "Are you my Tyya, caribou-bou-bou?"

When he reached the white animal, he threw the magic objects on its back.

Instantly the caribou changed into a woman. Into Tyya!

Etosack invited Tyya back to his tent and they lived together happily. His brothers put up a tent of their own nearby.

Tyya still collected pieces of wood and antler for her dollmaking. Whenever she saw caribou, she thought of the time when she had been one of them, the most beautiful caribou in the herd.

And ever since, when hunters meet a white caribou they treat it kindly and do not kill it, for it might be enchanted.

Elizabeth Cleaver Talks About Shadow Puppets

When I found the story of "The Enchanted Caribou" I thought how well it was suited to shadow puppets, since the shadow theatre is ideal for showing dreams, visions, and magical happenings like a human turning into an animal. A few years before, I had visited Baker Lake, west of Hudson Bay, and taught the children there how to make shadow puppets. How I wished I had known the story of "The Enchanted Caribou" then, because my friends Mary, Ruth, Jane, and Victor would have loved making their own shadow puppets to illustrate it.

The illustrations in this book can be made by anyone. I cut out of black paper the figures representing Tyya, Etosack and his brothers, the tent, and many caribou. I then arranged them on large sheets of white paper, making a new arrangement for each page of the story. What you see in this book are these figures when they were placed behind a lighted screen and photographed from the other side.

Of course in this book the figures cannot move. I will tell you how to make your own shadow-puppet theatre in which they *can* move. You might want to tell your own story with shadow figures. But here is a way to re-create the story of "The Enchanted Caribou".

HOW TO PREPARE YOUR SHADOW PLAY

1. Read *The Enchanted Caribou* several times so that you are familiar with it. (Or you could choose a different story, or a poem.)
2. List the characters you will have to cut out. There should be very few.
3. List each scene you will have to illustrate.
4. Decide on the scenery. It should be very simple.

EQUIPMENT

The most important things to have for a shadow performance are light, shadow figures, and a screen made of tracing paper or a white sheet. You will also have to use:

pencil and drawing paper
scissors
black paper
black bristol board
beading wire #34 (for connecting parts of a small figure)
paper fasteners (for connecting parts of a large figure)
drinking straws (to manipulate small figures)
wooden rods or dowels (to manipulate large figures)
masking tape (to fasten the straw to the shadow figure)
nylon thread (to manipulate birds etc.)
flashlight or 100-watt light bulb
thumb tacks

CREATING THE SHADOW FIGURES

1. Draw the shadow figures in profile on white paper and cut them out.
2. Once you are pleased with them, use these figures as patterns to cut out duplicates from black paper.
3. With scissors separate the head, arms, and legs of your figures. Then join them to the body with wire or paper fasteners.
4. For manipulation use drinking straws as rods and tape them to whatever you want to move—the arms, the legs, or the head.

THE SHADOW THEATRE

Your shadow theatre can be made from black bristol board. Cut out an opening and cover the back with tracing paper, fastening the paper with tape. You will sit behind this small screen, with a flashlight in front of you so that your hands are free to manipulate the shadow figures.

OR

For a large shadow screen, stretch a sheet or thin white cloth over a wooden frame and fasten the corners with thumb tacks. The light bulb should be placed centrally, two or three feet from behind the screen. The light should be high enough to prevent shadows from the operator's head being thrown onto the screen.

I hope you have as much fun with shadow puppets as I have had.

ELIZABETH CLEAVER